Hope for the Honeybees

Heal the Planet Book 1

by Kesi Augustine
Illustrated by Aranahaj Iqbal
Cover text by Bobooks

ISBN: 154128268X
ISBN-13: 978-1541282681

To my family.
With love,
     your "Kesi Bee."

What are bees good for? I get them everywhere.

>Bees on my clothes, and bees in my hair.

>Bees in my house, and bees at the park.

>Bees in the morning, and bees when its dark!

I think that bees are loud and mean. But bees want to be near me, even while I scream.

Bees on my clothes, bees in my hair, bees find me everywhere!

"Shoo!" I say when I swat them away. "Leave me alone!"

One summer day, I get a bee in my shoe. I hop and I jump. I wiggle and I jiggle.

But the bee stays tucked between my toes. "Buzz!" she says in her high-pitched voice.

"Ugh!" I shout. My voice quivers. "Go away!"

Finally, with one strong kick, I toss my shoe across the room. It hits the floor with a loud *thud.*

Mama opens the door.

"Hope! What's wrong?" she asks. "I can hear you carrying on from the kitchen."

"It's a bee!" I exclaim. "*Again*! Bees on my clothes, bees in my hair, bees find me everywhere!"

The bee floats in the air, buzzing loud and proud.

Mama laughs and playfully rolls her eyes. "Bees love you," she says.

"Well, I don't love them!" I pout. "Get it away from me!"

"Okay, okay. I'll let her out," Mama replies. She walks to the window.

I put a pillow over my head.

"Don't worry," Mama says. "She's just as afraid as you."

She opens the sunny window.

"Buzz! Buzz!" the bee says.

Mama knows how to make lullabies out of jibberish. She sings in her high sweet voice,
Bumblebee, honey bee, oh how I love thee...

I hold my breath and watch as the bee flies up, up, up. She bumps against the glass. Buzz. Buzz. Buzz. She sounds even louder.

Finally, the bee zooms outside.

Mama closes the window. The room sounds extra silent without the bee's buzz. My ears are ringing.

"We've gotta tell Dad to seal up the cracks in here," I say, letting my pillow drop to the floor. "What are bees good for, anyway?"

Mama smiles and shakes her head. "It's sealed. Plus, we're on the 5th floor. Bees fly high in the sky. And you know, Hope, bees aren't so bad. Maybe next time we can open the window together?"

I roll my eyes. "Maybe next lifetime."

Mama laughs.

That night, bees come to me in a dream.

There are rows and rows of flowers, both big and small, of every beautiful color. Swarms of bees float from flower to flower. Their buzzing sounds like an orchestra.

A bee lands on my arm. Then another, on my nose. And another, in my hair!

Bees on my clothes, bees in my hair, bees find me everywhere –

But in my dream, I don't shoo them away. Where I was once scared, I stand proud. I see their tiny legs, their proud chests, and their furry little hairs, yellow with pollen. I hear their flapping wings as they dance around my room.

Suddenly, I hear a high-pitched voice.

Hi Hope, it says.

I look down, and there's a bee on my hand.

What? I can hear bees talk?

Hi! I say, using the voice in my heart. Woah! I can also talk back!

We love you, Hope! the orchestra of buzzing bees sings to me. As I look up, a bee flies into my forehead.

The dream ends. I wake up with my heart racing.

The next day, while I'm sitting in the park, I take a bite out of an apple. A bee lands on the fruit.

I watch her closely. When I stare into her big eyes, I hear her whisper,

I'm hungry.

When she's finished with her snack, she flies away.

"That's weird," I say. I take another bite of the apple. "But it sure is delicious."

During my walk home, a bee hovers around my head. I hold my breath, and she lands on my shoulder. I stop in my tracks. My heart beats heavy like a drum.

I hear her whisper,

I'm so sleepy.

The bee rests for a moment, then flies away.

Later, I find two bees chasing each other near my apartment. Buzzing as loud as can be.

This time, I'm almost too afraid to go inside.

"Maybe I'll wait for Dad to get home," I say, "I can wait at the library."

I hear a small voice. This time, its in my heart.

We're afraid. We're far from home
and we've lost our dear friend, Lila.

What could *they* be afraid of? I wonder.

I place my hand over my heart. I sing my mom's song.
Bumblebee, honey bee, oh how I love
thee...

Just like that, the bees fly away.

When I get inside, Mama asks about my day.

"The weirdest thing happened in the park," I say. "A bee landed on my apple!"

Mama adds a few drops of honey to her tea. She has a big smile on her face. "Hm," she replies, "I wonder why she would do that?"

I pause, waiting to see if she will share her secret.

Mama is silent. She just keeps smiling. Her finger points toward my bedroom.

I run into my room. I turn on my computer to search for information about bees.

What are bees good for? I type.

At first, I learn that there's over twenty thousand different types of bees in the world! Sweat bees, carpenter bees, bumble bees. Some bees look like flying teddy bears.

You couldn't catch me near one of those! I think.

Then, I see a picture of a honeybee. These are the bees I get everywhere - in my clothes and in my hair.

I learn that honeybees are hard workers. They live to serve their colony, their queen, and our flowers.

Each bee has a specific job in their hive.

There's the queen, who lays eggs.
The male drones, who mate with the queen.
And the female workers, who do so many things – from cleaning, to caring for the larvae (baby bees), to guarding the hive, and, of course, flying from flower to flower, in search of enough pollen and nectar to feed the hive.

I also learn that honeybees are built for their work.

Their five eyes see the world as ripples of movement, and shades of purples and blues. These eyes can read the sun like a book, using its ultraviolet rays for direction.

And even though their wings make such a loud buzz, the wings of honeybees are actually too small for their bodies! The wings work by creating an extra lift to keep honeybees soaring high.

But when a honeybee feels threatened, watch out. She will give you a painful sting!

Bees evolved with flowers. As flowers changed their sizes and shapes, so did the bees.

Flowers offer bees pollen and nectar. In return, bees pollinate flowers.

When bees spread pollen, they fertilize crop plants. These crop plants create fruits and vegetables.

We eat these crops for vitamins and nutrients.

Honeybees can also transform the nectar from millions of flowers into one jar of sticky sweet honey.

People have loved honey for thousands of years. So do hungry bears, beetles, and badgers.

Not only is honey wonderfully delicious, it can help us to heal our bruises and burns.

But is honey for us, or just for the bees? Not everyone agrees.

Then I discover that honeybees are dying.

I see pictures of beekeepers with empty hives. Beekeepers have been finding ghost towns where their beehives used to be.

At first, 1/3 of their bees vanished without a trace. They left behind nothing. Sometimes, brokenhearted beekeepers would find a few larvae, the queen bee, and, of course, their honey. There were no signs of hungry bears, mites, or chemicals.

Year after year, bees continue to disappear.

But why?

> Maybe the bees are suffering from disease? Maybe we have cut down too many flowers and trees?

> Maybe there are too many poisons and mites, or maybe we are working the bees for too many days and nights?

> Could it be there's too much pollution in the air? Or that the globe has too much heat for bees to bear?

Or maybe its not the loss of flowers,
but the energies coming from cell phone towers?

Some people say yes. Some people say no.

Some people say we will never know.

Bees have buzzed on earth for 65 million years. And now they are falling off flowers. And vanishing from their hives.

"This world is too cold for them," I say sadly, closing my computer. I remember the honeybees that I saw today. They were hungry, tired, and afraid.

The bees are in pain.

Without honeybees, we won't have most fruits, or vegetables, or honey, or almonds, or even cotton.

I imagine not being able to eat my favorite apples. Then I remember how I kicked my shoe and almost hurt a honeybee. Just because I was afraid.

A tear falls down my cheek.

I lay down to sleep,
and make a wish for the bees.

"May the bees be safe," I whisper.
"May they be loved.
May we serve them,
as they have served
us."

The stars twinkle
outside my window.

When I wake up the next morning, there is a message in my heart.

I remember the stories of people who are working to save the honeybees. The beekeepers, the scientists, the artists, and even the kids like me!

During breakfast, I explain what I learned to Mama.

She watches me with a smile on her face.

"So, you want to build a honeybee kingdom?" she asks. She adds a spoonful of honey to her tea.

"Yes! We could make a garden in the sky!" I shout, spilling some milk on the table. "We could have sunflowers, and lilies, and maybe even tomatoes! As much as we can fit on the roof. Everyone in the building can help."

"Well, let's take the day to come up with our plan," Mama says, sipping her tea, "And we'll reconvene at dinner."

A few moments later, I am drawing in the park. The sun is hanging hot in the sky.

I've got a picture of the flowers we can put on our roof. It's a small start. But bees can come and go as they please.

I'll be there, too, with bees on my clothes, and bees in my hair.

As I draw the petals on a yellow sunflower, a honeybee lands on my hand.

I hear her small voice say,

Thank you.

The decline of our bees results from a complex web of factors that mostly result from modern advances in technology. Colony Collapse Disorder (CCD) has been puzzling scientists around the world since 2006. All of Hope's research is based on facts from books and films about the disappearance of bees. Although Hope learns specifically about honeybees, many of the world's bee species have declined during the past 50 years.

What can we do to help the honeybees?

1) Use *Hope for the Honeybees* as a starting point for your own research on the dangers that honeybees currently face. You might start with a book on honeybees, Colony Collapse Disorder, or articles on beekeeper Dave Hackenberg (who discovered twenty million of his honey bees were missing in 2006) and Michelle Obama's vegetable garden (which brought the first bee hives to the White House of the United States).

2) Do you have a small lawn or windowsill? Plant flowers or vegetables that honeybees love. Make sure to keep your plants free of insecticides and other harsh chemicals. These chemicals can negatively affect the memory and immune systems of bees for generations.

3) If you choose to continue eating honey (like Hope's Mama), consider buying local honey from a farmer's market or a grocery store.

4) Learn about the young activists and entrepreneurs like Mikaila Ulmer who are working to help honeybees. What information have they shared about honeybees? In what ways might you be able to support their organizations?

5) "Be Like a Bee": Follow the example of honeybees. In what ways can you cooperate with your family? What special talents do you have that make you happy? How might these gifts also help your community?

Author's Note

I have always had a special relationship with honeybees: they chase me, and I tear off running. Like Hope (who I named after my beloved grandmother), I have had bees in my hair, in my apartment, and even in my shoes.

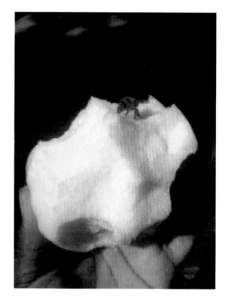

A bee friend visits me during a summer afternoon.

As I've grown older, I have encountered people who are also terrified of honeybees. And I've learned from the people who are in awe of them. These bee lovers inspired me to do my own research, and I quickly learned about the work that all bees do for the planet.

I also learned about Colony Collapse Disorder. Since 2006, this phenomenon has left beekeepers and scientists alike stunned about the silent yet dramatic disappearance of honeybees. Beekeeper Gunther Hauk writes in *Toward Saving the Honeybees* (2002) that the bee "is a sick patient who has been trying for years to signal to us the deep crises of its diminishing life forces and its increasing inability to resonate with the environment" (p. 10). Unfortunately, we have statistical evidence for Hauk's claims: According to director Markus Imhoof of *More Than Honey* (2013), 50 to 90 percent of local bees have disappeared worldwide. Meanwhile, we need bees to pollinate 80 percent of our plants.

I realized that we rely on the diligent service of bees to sustain us, and I began to see honeybees as powerful yet vulnerable little creatures. I conquered my fear of honeybees by opening my heart to them.

The honeybees, and child activists, inspired me to write this book. I am humbled by the love, compassion, and cosmic imaginations of today's children. My Heal the Planet series aims to show all that all children are the heroes of the world.

Thank you to Kyle Martin for reading an early draft of the manuscript. A special thank you to the wonderful women who embraced me and encouraged my writing of *Hope for the Honeybees* during our potluck dinner: Amy Ellks, Taryn Hughes, Monica Polanco, Deborah Schaeffer, and Lori Schroeter. May 2017 be filled with the sweetness of honey for you all. And thank you especially to my hive of ancestors for your unconditional love.   --KAA

Learn More About Honeybees!

Books

<u>The Bee Crisis</u>

Honey Bees: Letters from the Hive by Steve Buchmann (Delacorte Press, 2010)

The Hive Detectives: Chronicle of a Honey Bee Catastrophe by Loree Griffin Burns (Houghton Mifflin, 2010).

Magic School Bus: Inside a Beehive by Joanna Cole (Scholastic Press, 1996).

The Hive Detectives: Chronicle of a Honey Bee Catastrophe by Loree Griffin Burns (Houghton Mifflin Books for Children, 2010)

The Honey Makers by Gail Gibbons (Morrow Junior Books, 1997)

The Fascinating World Of... Bees by Angel Julivert (Barron's Educational Series, 1991)

The Case of the Vanishing Honeybees: A Scientific Mystery by Sandra Markle (Millbrook Press, 2014)

The Bee: A Natural History by Noah Wilson-Rich (Princeton University Press, 2014)*

Be Like a Bee by Seta Simonian (Rosedog Books, 2012)

The Buzz on Bees: Why Are They Disappearing? by Shelley Rother and Anne Woodhull (Holiday House, 2010)

Honey Lovers

The Big Honey Hunt by Stan Bernstain (Random House, 1962)

The Honeybee and the Robber by Eric Carle (Philomel Books, 2001)

Winnie the Pooh by A.A. Milne (E.P. Dutton, 1926)

Documentaries

Disneynature: Wings of Life (Disneynature Backlight Films, 2011)

Vanishing of the Bees (dir. Maryam Henein & George Langworthy, 2009)

More Than Honey (dir. Markus Imhoof, 2013)

The Bees of Transylvania (dir. Paul E. Visser, 2014)

Websites and Articles

ACT for Bees – http://actforbees.org/resources/

Me & the Bees Lemonade - http://www.meandthebees.com/

Mikaila Ulmer's Google talk about her company, Me & the Bees, on YouTube.

https://www.youtube.com/watch?v=1H4R5e64NDE

"White House Bees: Meet the first hive" by Jeff Simon, *CNN*, November 17, 2015. http://www.cnn.com/2015/10/15/politics/white-house-beekeeper-charlie-brandts/

About the Author

Kesi Augustine is a graduate student. She lives in Queens, New York with her pet bunnies.

Follow her Facebook for future updates in the Heal the Planet series: facebook.com/kesi.a.augustine

About the Illustrator

Aranahaj Iqbal is a freelance illustrator based in Pakistan. Visit her Facebook for more information about her work: facebook.com/massyartt

23953197R00022